WRITHE

HELLISH #14

CHARITY PARKERSON

—Warning: This book is intended for readers over the age of 18.

Copyright © 2021 Charity Parkerson
Editor: BZ Hercules & Consultants
Photographer: Dan Skinner
ISBN: 978-1-946099-91-4
All rights reserved.

INTRODUCTION

Dustin just wants to start over. Michael needs redemption. Together, they'll uncover a love written in the stars.

When Dustin's life undergoes a major upheaval, he embraces the change and moves to the middle of nowhere. His small historic home quickly goes from a private respite to a no-one-can-hear-him-scream mystery. Feelings of being watched, unexplained touches, and voices send him on a hunt for answers. The more he uncovers, the stranger things get until Dustin finds himself entrenched in a world he didn't know existed. Now he doesn't know if he can escape.

Michael was exiled more years ago than he can count. Life has continued on without him. Over the millennia, Michael has embraced the silence and loneliness. It's possible he passed into madness at some point. Then Dustin arrives, bringing noise into his solitude. He can't let Dustin get away. Everything inside him screams Dustin is his destiny. First, he needs to convince Dustin he's real.

This time, when the Hellish clan finds itself sucked into the drama of their supernatural community, secrets will find their way into the light. No one is safe from the fallout.

ONE

JULY IN NEW ORLEANS was no joke. Dustin had grown up here. Still, he never got used to the humidity. Sweat poured down his body. No matter how much water he drank, he never felt hydrated. Even the darkness didn't bring relief. It was a good thing he lived in an old house in the middle of nowhere. There wasn't a chance in hell of him looking like anything but a swamp monster in this heat. While he wasn't a vain guy, he still wouldn't be caught dead in public with his clothes completely soaked in sweat. No one wanted to see his ass crack sweating through his jeans.

A small smile tugged at his lips. It was nighttime and in the middle of nowhere. Dustin could strip naked and sit on his porch swing. No one would know. At the thought, Dustin did just that. He laughed as he tossed every piece of clothing he wore toward the front door. This was exactly why Dustin had moved back out here. He craved solitude and the freedom this place gave him. Dustin plopped down on the swing and set it in motion. It felt so much better outside now. A slight breeze whipped through the porch and dried the sweat on his skin. Dustin tilted his chin up and closed his eyes, savoring the moment. He needed the little things. Dustin was relearning how to be happy.

Six months ago, Dustin hadn't known how to relax. His six-figure job with an investment firm and high-maintenance wife had demanded every ounce of him. Then Dustin had caught his wife fucking his boss and everything changed. Now he was divorced and free. Dustin cashed in every asset he possessed and moved into his grandparents' old house in the middle of nowhere. It was a life completely opposite to everything he had known since he graduated college. Dustin had been a slave to station and expectations for too many years. Now he wanted life to be quiet. It hurt less that way.

He swore fingers brushed through his hair. "Dustin."

Dustin's head shot up and eyes his flew open at the whisper. His gaze shot in every direction. There was no one. Dustin shook his head. He wondered if he had dozed off for a second. Dustin checked the time. It was almost midnight. He pushed to his feet and padded over to grab his clothes. It was no wonder he fell asleep or heard things. He had been up since six a.m., unpacking boxes and cleaning up the brush around the outside of the house. Dustin was dirty and tired. He needed a shower and sleep.

As he stepped inside, Dustin dropped his clothes by the door and then locked the front door behind him. A sense of peace and pride built inside him as his gaze skirted the room. The place was an open design with all wood flooring. Everything was on one level, and he could see into each room from the front door. Even though the house was over a hundred years old, Dustin had updated everything. His high efficiency refrigerator had a light in the ice maker that looked just like a nightlight in the otherwise dark kitchen. A lamp in the living room also kept the place from being completely plunged into darkness. Shadows seemed to move sometimes, catching Dustin off guard. He wasn't used to the absolute darkness of country living anymore. The frogs and crickets kept the silence at bay, but not by much. Dustin had gotten used to streetlights and traffic over the past fifteen years. This house was isolated from the world. At night, it felt doubly secluded. He didn't recall feeling that way as a child, but life had changed, and the house had sat empty for too long. Dustin wasn't used to being alone. He had to push that final bit from his mind. Things were better this way.

Dustin shook off the feeling of the darkness watching him and headed for the bathroom inside his bedroom. Since Dustin had a tankless water heater installed before he moved in, it took a little longer for the water to heat. He stared at his reflection in the full-length mirror while he waited. At thirty-five, life had caught him up with him more than he liked. He had always thought of himself as being just average, but the stress of the divorce had him looking ragged as hell. There were dark smudges beneath his hazel eyes. His curly blond hair had gotten shaggier than usual. He kind of liked it that way. To be honest, despite his less than perfect appearance, he liked himself better now. His ex-wife, Amanda, had been his high-school sweetheart. They had drifted apart the last few years. It had almost been a relief when he caught her with Christian. But their divorce had been like most, ugly as hell. Now he felt changed in some way he couldn't explain. He had worked for years to give Amanda everything she wanted, but it hadn't been enough. Dustin didn't know how to go back to feeling like he was enough for anyone now. Still, without her and the job that had been slowly killing him, Dustin finally felt at peace. He brushed and flossed, trying not to think about the past. Dustin wanted to go straight to bed after his shower and keep putting days between the past and himself. This was the life he wanted now.

Something stirred in the corner of Dustin's vision in the mirror's reflection. Dustin spun. Nothing was there. He turned back and that corner of the mirror slowly fogged. Dustin shook his head. He was such a dumbass, letting the mirror steaming over scare him. Obviously, the water had heated while he had been distracted. Dustin blew off his uneasiness and climbed into the shower.

Hot water poured down Dustin's body. He laughed at his ridiculousness as he shampooed his hair. The change of scenery messed with him more than he expected. He had known the place would be quiet. Dustin hadn't expected the isolation would have him jumping at every tiny thing. He got clean while trying not to think too much about it. One thing Dustin noticed in the two weeks he had been living here was he could easily spook himself. This was such an old house. It was easy to think of it as haunted. The floors creaked and doors opened with no one there. Drafts pulled them closed again. Even though he didn't believe in ghosts, he had to admit this place could be a little creepy at night.

Once clean, Dustin stepped from the shower and dried his body. He tossed his towel in the hamper and then headed for the living room to grab the clothes he had left by the door. They were gone. Dustin retraced his steps again. The clothes were in the hamper. Dustin moved back to the living room and stared at the spot where he had dropped the clothes earlier. He had left the clothes right here, right? There was a long, fluffy-looking white feather on the floor. Dustin bent and picked it up. The moment his fingers touched the feather, a sense of peace washed over him. Dustin was being weird again. He was so tired. Dustin had already dozed off outside. Of course, he had carried the clothes to the hamper and forgotten. It wasn't like anyone else could have done it.

Dustin stared at the feather he held as he headed for bed. He wondered where it came from. As far as he had seen, there weren't any swans or geese or anything like that around. The feather almost had a shimmer to it—like it had been doused in glitter. It was pretty. Dustin had never seen one like it. He set it on the nightstand by the bed. His gaze never wavered from it as he slipped between the covers nude. He stared at the feather until his eyelids grew heavy. As his eyes fell closed, an odd thought overcame him. Maybe he had an angel watching over him.

For two weeks, Michael watched Dustin pad around the house, looking for ways to keep busy. Even if Michael couldn't hear Dustin's thoughts, he would know the guy was used to working all day. Dustin desperately wanted this quiet life. He simply didn't know how to be at peace. His mind was too loud. Michael couldn't get enough of watching him, hearing him, and trying to help. He recalled exactly how he had felt when he had been exiled. Dustin could leave. Michael couldn't. He would pray for his only slice of human interaction to stay forever, but Michael knew better. The only person who might hear his prayers was the same person who had banished him to this prison with no bars. Watching Dustin now, he understood why Celeste had done it. Michael couldn't control the hunger.

Angels weren't supposed to interact. Not the way Michael wanted. They were silent protectors. Warriors for the heavens. Michael looked at humans and he wanted what they had: freedom. He wanted the scent of carnival food, the sun beating on his face, and the shaky feeling in his stomach from a roller coaster. Michael wanted the sand between his toes and soft kisses on his lips. He was a glutton for life. Dustin reminded him of all those things.

Part of Michael recognized Celeste had likely sent Dustin to him as a test. If he touched him, Dustin might disappear, and Michael would get another thousand years of exile. It was worth it. He snagged the corner of Dustin's blanket and tugged, working it down Dustin's body. Dustin rolled onto his back and covered his eyes with his arm. Michael froze, waiting him out. While Dustin couldn't see Michael unless Michael let him; he still needed Dustin asleep. Otherwise, Dustin might run away. Michael wasn't ready to go back to being alone yet.

Dustin didn't move. Michael went back to slowly dragging the covers away until he had Dustin's entire body exposed. Yum. Like all humans, Dustin was perfect in Michael's eyes. He was a work of art. His heart had been slightly damaged from the stress of a cheating spouse. If left untreated, he would develop an arrhythmia, shortening his life. He also had an ulcer and arthritis in his knees. Michael set his hand on Dustin's thigh and healed him. Even if Celeste took him away, Michael needed to know Dustin was okay. He would live a long life.

With Dustin healed, the warm skin beneath his palm caught and held Michael's attention. It had been so long since he had touched anyone. He couldn't move his hand away. Dustin's full lips parted. He sighed. The sound stirred Michael's cock. Before he could stop himself, he dove into Dustin's dreams. They were disjointed. He was flying, but the scenery kept changing—like Dustin couldn't focus on what sight he wanted to see most, so everything was a blur. Michael wrapped his arms around Dustin mid-flight, slowing things down. He showed Dustin the whales playing in the ocean. From there, he jumped to the desert, showing Dustin how even the barren nothingness could be beautiful. They flew to the seven wonders of the world and saw every continent. Finally, they landed in Michael's favorite spot. The grassy knolls of Ireland where leprechauns hid. Color surrounded them. Blue, purple, orange, and green. The place looked like a living rainbow.

Dustin looked around with wonder written on his face. Finally, his gaze landed on Michael. "Am I dead?"

A smile pulled at Michael's lips. "No. You're dreaming."

Dustin's gaze shifted to Michael's wings. "I found a feather earlier. Was it yours?"

Michael nodded. "I'm sorry if I scared you. You were so tired. I thought I would make things easier by picking up your clothes."

Dustin's hand lifted. He paused. His gorgeous gaze met Michael's. "Is it okay if I touch them?"

Michael turned slightly, giving Dustin easier access to his wings. "It's your dream."

When Dustin caressed his wings, Michael ground his back teeth, fighting a moan. Dustin had no idea what he did to Michael. Being stroked was ecstasy. Being alone was madness. He longed for more of Dustin.

"You're beautiful."

At Dustin's compliment, Michael's gaze shot to his. "You are too."

Dustin blushed. "I don't think I've ever had another man say that to me."

"I'm not a man. I'm an angel. Does that bother you, though? Having another man compliment you, I mean."

For a moment, Dustin seemed to think it over. Finally, he shook his head. "It's nice. I don't think anyone has said anything kind to me in years. I'll take what I can get." The smile that accompanied that confession had Michael biting back another moan.

"Maybe don't look at it like that."

Dustin's eyebrows rose at the suggestion. "How should I look at it, then?"

Michael inched closer, invading Dustin's space a little more. "Think of how a man could pleasure you. A man would know all the hot spots because he has them too."

They held each other's stare. Dustin didn't back down. "I thought you weren't a man."

A smile that felt evil even to Michael stretched his lips. "I didn't say we were talking about me, but I'm glad to know I'm who you pictured, and you're right. The things I could do for you would blow even your wildest fantasies away. You'd never want anyone else ever again."

The edges of Dustin's dream darkened, and Michael knew their time was ending.

Dustin cast a desperate look around, as if he knew it too. His gaze shot back to Michael's. "Tell me your name."

Before Michael responded, Dustin sat up in bed, blinking. Michael stayed hidden, watching. Dustin's gaze landed on Michael. Michael's lips parted. He swore Dustin could see him. The hairs on Michael's arms stood. Then it was over. Dustin gathered his blankets and settled down again. Michael released the breath he hadn't known he had been holding. They would see each other again. Consequences be damned.

TWO

THE FIELDS around Dustin's house were starting to look a little less unkempt. He had invested in a small utility tractor for moving and clearing brush. It had taken him a bit of practice to learn how best to use it. Now that Dustin had it figured out, his acreage was slowly looking better.

He drove the tractor in circles while poring over a dream he kept having. Dreams supposedly had underlying meanings. If so, Dustin really wanted to get to the bottom of this one. He felt better than he had in ages, but he had a bad feeling he was dead in his dreams. There was no other reason for the angel to always be there, showing him the world. If it wasn't a dream about dying, Dustin feared he was questioning his sexuality. He had never looked at another man sexually before. Now he couldn't stop thinking about the guy in his dreams. Dustin never learned his name.

Too many times a day to count, Dustin caught himself staring into space, picturing the man in his dreams. Before recently, Dustin couldn't recall ever seeing anyone as clearly. Usually, his dreams were pretty vague. This guy was as clear as Dustin's reflection in the mirror. He had these blue eyes that were the same color as the sky on a bright summer's day. Yet his hair was as black as night. If he didn't have wings, Dustin swore he still would have known he was an angel. He wasn't the chubby blond-haired cherubs of paintings. This guy was the tall, beautiful warriors of legend. Dustin couldn't put him out of his head.

This morning had been the worst one so far. Dustin had lain awake, incapable of getting out of bed. All his thoughts had been consumed by the blue-eyed angel. His hand had slipped beneath the covers without thought. The angel's erotic promises filled Dustin's chest. Never, not one time in his entire life had Dustin jacked off to the fantasy of a man. Maybe this divorce had sucker-punched him harder than he thought. Dustin had zero desire to ever be with another woman. In fact, he didn't want anyone except his dream man. Dustin wanted him to have a name.

A movement caught Dustin's eye and pulled him from his spiraling thoughts. A man in a white V-neck t-shirt and jeans made his way toward Dustin. His jet-black hair fell to his shoulders. He gave Dustin a small wave as Dustin killed the tractor.

"Hey."

At Dustin's greeting, the guy smiled. Perfect straight white teeth coupled with deep lines at the corner of his mouth hit Dustin first. Then Dustin saw his eyes. An angel's eyes. His angel's eyes.

"Hey, there. I heard a rumor that someone had bought this house. When I heard the tractor going, I decided to come say hi. I'm your closest neighbor."

It was the man from his dreams. There could be no mistake. He didn't have wings, but it was him. Dustin stumbled a bit as he climbed from the tractor. He couldn't believe his eyes. Dustin covered up his misstep by pausing to wipe his palms on his jeans. "Oh. It's good to meet you. I'm Dustin." He held his hand out to shake.

As the man's hand enveloped Dustin's, a spark of electricity traveled up his arm before hitting his heart. "I'm Michael."

His name was Michael. Dustin couldn't stop staring at him like an idiot. He swallowed and tried tearing his gaze away. It didn't happen. Dustin was held hostage. "I didn't know I had any neighbors."

Michael's smile grew. It got a little harder to breathe. "I have a cabin in the woods behind you. You can only get to it by boat."

A soft laugh escaped Dustin. "That explains why I haven't seen the place. It sounds like you might be an even bigger hermit than me."

"Maybe. It's just been me for a long time, so I suppose that's true."

He was beautiful. Dustin forced his gaze toward the house. The guy probably thought he was a weirdo. "Would you like a beer or something?"

"Sure."

At Michael's agreement, Dustin found his gaze sliding back toward Michael. Michael stared back with an intensity and kindness Dustin had never experienced. Except for his dreams, that is. He couldn't shake that. Dustin was completely positive this was the same man. He had dreamed of this guy before meeting him. It felt... serendipitous.

They headed for the front of the house. Dustin had a cooler full of beer on the steps. He felt Michael's gaze following him as he popped the lid and grabbed two longnecks. Dustin passed one Michael's way and moved to sit on the porch swing. Michael twisted off the cap and leaned against the porch railing.

"I've always liked this old house. It's been sitting empty for a while now."

Dustin nodded and set the swing in motion. "This was my grandparents' place. I grew up here. I inherited everything when they passed several years ago, but my wife... ex-wife," Dustin corrected, "didn't want to move out of the city. When we got divorced, I decided this would be a great place to start over."

Michael nodded along as if he understood. "Do you plan to stay for good, or is this just a resting spot until you figure out your next move?"

"I'm staying put." Even Dustin heard the fierce note in his voice. He tried reeling it back in so he didn't sound so bitter. "I have a lot of plans for the place. When I'm done, it'll look as good as new." He hated he was the only one talking about himself. Dustin needed to know more about this man who had been in his dreams. "Tell me about yourself. Are you married? Do you have kids?" Dustin prayed the man had a wife and twelve kids, so maybe Dustin could stop looking at him in a way that made Dustin uncomfortable as hell.

Michael moved to join Dustin on the swing. Their knees touched. "No wife. I have two sons, but they're grown. Being career military and a single dad doesn't mix. They were raised mostly by my grandmother and trusted friends. I'm not sure they even know I exist."

Damn. Dustin felt that deeper than he could say. "I used to work my ass off nonstop, thinking I would retire early, and my ex-wife and I could travel the world. The whole time, she was fucking my boss, so I get it. I'm pretty sure she didn't know I existed."

Michael flashed him a smile. "What do you do now? Are you finally enjoying that early retirement?"

"I am." Even Dustin heard the happiness in his voice. "Between selling everything we owned and lots of smart investing over the years, I'm finally free." With Michael sitting so close, Dustin couldn't help but stare. Michael didn't look old enough to have two grown sons. "How old are you?" The question popped out before Dustin could help it. He tried explaining his rudeness. "It's just that you said you were career military and have two grown sons. You don't look a day over twenty-eight." Dustin swore, as he looked on, laugh lines appeared in the corners of Michael's eyes.

A sexy smile stretched Michael's lips. "I come from good genes. You should see my grandmother. She looks so young, she'll have you questioning everything you know." Before Dustin could point out Michael hadn't answered him, Michael draped his arm across the back of the swing. All Dustin's thoughts died. Michael wasn't touching him, but Dustin could feel his heat. Smell him. Dustin fought to keep his eyes open. Michael smelled like something sweet Dustin couldn't place. Nostalgia washed over him. He wanted to bury his face against Michael's skin and inhale. He was irresistible.

Michael kept talking, oblivious to the way he drove Dustin wild. "You said you have a lot of plans for the place. Paint me a picture."

Dustin grabbed the topic like a life preserver. "I'm clearing out that field for a garden. I haven't decided what I'm growing yet. Probably mostly vegetables, but I need to test the soil. There's a huge stump I need pulled out of the ground, but I'm hoping to do some tall plants and a koi pond at the edge of the porch."

Michael sat forward and slapped Dustin's knee. "Show me the stump. I might be able to help."

Dustin jumped to his feet. He was beyond grateful for any excuse to move away from Michael. Dustin currently rocked a semi, and he had no idea what was happening to his head. He would do anything for a distraction. Dustin led Michael to the stump. They spent several minutes discussing the best way to remove it before moving on to Dustin's design ideas. Before Dustin knew it, he had a notebook and pen, drawing a rough sketch of the garden and pond. Michael nodded along and gave several helpful suggestions. They ended up testing the soil in several places and drawing up plans for each section of various fruits and vegetables. In no time at all, the sun dipped low in the sky. He checked his watch.

"Damn. I kept you all day."

Michael shrugged. "I've enjoyed myself. Plus, I have nothing else going on. Maybe I can come back tomorrow, and we can get started on the pond."

Dustin wasn't ready for Michael to leave. He rushed to keep him a little longer. "Would you like to stay for dinner? I've had chicken and dumplings cooking in the crockpot all day. It should be ready."

"I'd like that."

At Michael's agreement, Dustin nodded. While fighting a smile, he led Michael back toward the house. At the edge of the porch, he grabbed the cooler. Side by side, they toed off their shoes by the door and headed inside. Dustin set the cooler on the counter and they took turns washing their hands. They moved together seamlessly, as if they had been eating together for years. Dustin set the table. Michael unpacked the cooler and dumped the mostly melted ice in the sink. After putting the beer away, Michael found the pitcher of sweet tea and poured each of them a glass. Dustin filled their plates and carried them to the table. It was nice. Their conversation was never stilted. Dustin talked about living in the city and getting no sleep. Michael told him about his first few years of living in a secluded cabin in the woods. Dustin related with a lot of Michael's experiences. They had both felt disoriented and aimless their first few nights.

With their plates scraped clean, they headed for the sink. Michael put the leftovers away while Dustin filled the sink with soapy water. They hadn't dirtied a ton of dishes, but Dustin's breakfast dishes had still been in the sink too. Side by side, they cleaned. Dustin washed and Michael dried. As Dustin shoved a bottle brush inside a cup, bubbles shot out and hit him in the face. They laughed as Michael wiped them away. Then their gazes met. Dustin held his breath. They were too close. Michael hovered over him and Dustin couldn't look away. There was so much heat between them, Dustin couldn't think. Michael lowered his head.

Dustin jumped away before their lips could meet. "Whoa. No. Just wait. I don't swing that way." The claim was out there before Dustin had time to think.

Michael looked away. He set the dish towel on the counter. "I'm sorry. I guess I..." He walked away, heading for the door.

Dustin stared after him, trapped in his confusion. He had wanted that kiss. Michael hadn't misread things. Dustin was the bastard. His body finally unfroze as the front door closed behind Michael. Dustin chased after him.

"Michael. Wait. It's not your..." Dustin stared at the empty porch in confusion. Michael was gone. Dustin scanned the yard and field in the direction where Michael had appeared that morning. There was no sign of him anywhere. Dustin scrubbed at his forehead in frustration as he headed back inside. He was such a fucking idiot. Dustin had spent the entire day mooning at Michael, touching him as much as possible, and holding eye contact way longer than necessary. What had he expected? He hadn't even gotten Michael's number. Dustin had no way to apologize or explain. Fuck. He was such an asshole.

Dustin stomped his way back to the sink. He would finish cleaning the kitchen, take a shower, and go to bed. Maybe tomorrow he would head out the direction Michael had appeared from and see if he could find Michael's cabin. He didn't know what he would say if he found Michael, but he had to try. Dustin froze as he reached the sink. All the dishes were gone. The dish towel Michael had tossed aside was now neatly folded next to the sink. His washcloth was draped over the middle of the double sink, drying. Even the crockpot had been put away. Nothing was as he left it. The sink had been full of soapy water and dirty dishes. Michael had definitely wadded up that towel and tossed it aside. This wasn't a matter of being upset or tired. His kitchen hadn't been clean, and now it was spotless.

He couldn't breathe. Something wasn't right. His gaze shot around the room. Was there someone there, hiding? He hurried around the house, turning on every light and checking every closet. Dustin left no room or corner unchecked. He was alone. There was no explanation for what happened. Maybe his house really was haunted. Was his grandmother still there? She had been a clean freak. Everything had its place. Dustin shook his head. That wasn't possible. Ghosts weren't real. He had to have misremembered. Dustin checked the locks and windows. With everything locked up tight, he headed for the shower. He needed to get some sleep. Tomorrow couldn't come soon enough. He wanted to see Michael. Dustin had to make this right.

THREE

MICHAEL GOT STARTED BEFORE SUNRISE. He didn't want Dustin to see him magically pulling a stump from the ground, but that was the easiest way to insert himself back into Dustin's life. Despite knowing all Dustin's thoughts, Michael wasn't good at deciphering them. He had known Dustin had never been touched by another man. Michael just didn't quite understand humans. Kisses weren't gendered. Life simply didn't work that way. Michael recognized human lives were fleeting, but he didn't understand why their thinking could be so small. The universe was so much bigger than they realized. With such short lives, he would think they would want to live them, but no. Too many of them chose to seal their lives in tiny boxes and never looked past the thin cardboard walls. It was ridiculous. Nonetheless, Michael wouldn't give up on Dustin. He knew Dustin felt something for him. Michael just needed to give him time.

After removing the stump, he snapped his fingers, making all the supplies for a new pond appear. He grabbed a shovel and pretended to work when he felt Dustin getting closer. The front door opened. Michael glanced up and wiped fake sweat from his brow.

"Good morning."

Dustin looked more than a little surprised to see Michael, but not disappointed. "Hey. Good morning. You got the stump out."

Michael leaned on his shovel and nodded. "I called a buddy of mine last night and he gave me a few tips. It came out pretty easy." He kept talking even as Dustin descended the steps and moved closer to inspect the hole. "I was thinking. You said you wanted the pond in the corner, but how about right here instead? There's already a hole from the stump and I had this stuff in my garage—"

"I'm sorry about last night."

Michael tried to blow off Dustin's apology and interruption. "It's not a big deal."

"It is to me," Dustin said, sounding determined. "I like you and I didn't mean to make things awkward. It's just that I've never kissed another man. Hell, I've never—"

Michael kissed Dustin, cutting off his excuses. He didn't give Dustin time to think. Michael simply overcame him and didn't hold back. He bit Dustin's bottom lip and then dove in the second Dustin's lips parted. Michael held Dustin's face and gave everything he had. He licked and sucked. His heart soared. It had been so long. So long. Everything ached. Michael's eyes burned. No one knew how he suffered. He didn't want to pull away, but he also didn't want to scare Dustin.

Michael wiped the moisture from Dustin's bottom lip. Dustin stared at him, looking floored. Michael took a step back. "There. You can never again say you haven't been kissed by a man. What do you think about my idea for the pond?"

Dustin blinked. He cleared his throat and glanced at the hole in the ground. "Yeah. I mean, that makes sense. It seems crazy to dig a second hole." He eyed all the things on the ground Michael had magicked to life. "Wow. All of this was in your garage?"

Michael tried acting nonchalant. "Yeah. I had thought about building a pond a few years back but never got around to it. All this stuff is just going to waste and taking up space, so I thought I could save you a few bucks."

Dustin moved some things around, inspecting the stone and fiberglass pond. "Wow. This is perfect. It looks to be the exact size I need and everything. This is great. Thank you."

Michael shrugged. "It's no big deal. Would you like to get started on it?"

"Maybe I could make you breakfast first?"

Since Michael didn't eat and had already faked it once, he shook his head. "I'm good. If you want to eat something and rejoin me afterward, I can get started without you."

Dustin shook his head. "No. I'm good. Just let me grab some coffee and we'll get started."

Michael watched him go with his heart in his throat. Now that the moment had passed, Michael fought to keep his teeth from chattering. The last time he had touched a human, Celeste's fury had been epic. He had been exiled to the middle of nowhere with zero contact with anyone. Michael didn't know why he was like this. His brothers and sisters were all content to play by the rules and stick with their own kind. Not Michael. He had this draw, pulling him to his grandmother's creation. Humans felt things deeper than anyone in the heavens. They weren't muted. Their passion was unmatched. Michael couldn't stop craving the chaos.

Dustin reappeared with a thermos of coffee and two cups. Side by side, they went to work. Halfway into their project, Dustin cast Michael a nervous look. "Um. Crazy question for you. Do you believe in ghosts?"

"Absolutely. Why?"

At Michael's quick response, Dustin's shoulders visibly relaxed. "I've had some weird things happening since I moved in, and I can't logic them away. It's just got me to thinking."

Michael kept working as he spoke, so Dustin wouldn't feel uncomfortable in his confessions. "Well, this is New Orleans. This land has seen a lot and had a ton of hoodoo and voodoo practiced here. Who knows what lingers? If you're feeling uncomfortable about it, there's a place in the Quarter. Baptiste's Voodoo Shoppe, I think is the name. They're the best for protection spells and cleansing. Whatever you need, they'll have it."

Dustin didn't respond right away. When Michael looked his way, he found Dustin staring at him. "Maybe I'll check it out," Dustin said after a moment. "I'm finding out a lot of things about myself lately. I'm not afraid to try something new."

There was no missing the double meaning behind Dustin's words. Michael was more than willing to be Dustin's guide into the unknown. After all, he had all the time in the world, and he needed a thousand more days like yesterday.

On the sly, Dustin kept touching his lips. He couldn't stop. His lips still tingled from Michael's rough kiss. Michael acted as if nothing happened while Dustin floundered. He wanted to do it again. As the pond came together, he felt his time with

Michael ticking away. Dustin couldn't let him get away.

"It looks like I'm already ready to add some fish. Would you like to go with me to pick some up? Maybe we could grab some dinner first."

Michael looked like he fought with himself. "I'd love to, but I have some PTSD issues. I don't really go to town. Maybe I can cook for you tomorrow night?"

Dustin would take what he could get. "I'd like that. Last night, I realized I don't have your number or know where you live." Dustin tried to stop there. He couldn't. "I worried I wouldn't see you again."

Michael swiped his hands on his jeans and pulled a phone from his back pocket. "We can't have that. What's your number?"

Dustin rattled off his number.

Michael nodded and typed on his phone. "Okay. I'm texting you GPS coordinates to my cabin. Basically, you can cut straight through the woods behind your house and run right into it, but I don't want you getting lost."

The phone buzzed in Dustin's pocket. He pulled it out and saved Michael's number. It took all of his willpower not to crow in triumph. Every second with Michael made Dustin felt like they were a little more tied together.

"Got it. Would you like something to drink for the walk home? It's pretty miserable out today."

Michael shoved his phone back in his pocket and motioned toward the house. "Lead the way. I'll take whatever you have to offer."

Dustin headed for the door with Michael on his heels. He glanced behind him, catching Michael staring at his ass. Michael smiled with zero guilt in his expression. Dustin pretended nothing happened, hoping to hide the pride growing in his chest. Even as a guy who had never dated men, he recognized how big of a catch Michael was. "I have bottled water, iced tea, and beer. You're welcome to anything you want."

I want you.

If Dustin hadn't been looking directly at Michael, he would have sworn Michael spoke to him. He hadn't. His lips never moved, yet the words had been loud as hell. They sounded exactly like the voice he had heard when he dozed off on the porch swing. Dustin glanced around.

"Did you hear that?"

"Hear what?"

Heat exploded through Dustin's face at the question. He couldn't repeat what he had heard. "Never mind. I swear the trees talk out here."

Dustin headed for the fridge, determined not to be strange for five minutes. Cool air washed over him when he opened the door. He stared at nothing, forgetting why he was there.

You're getting me a bottle of water.

"Oh yeah," Dustin said with a chuckle, grabbing two bottles. He passed one Michael's way. "Thanks for the reminder. I think I spaced out for a second. I must be more overheated than I realized."

As Michael reached for the bottle, he eyed Dustin with his eyebrows drawn together. "I didn't say anything."

Dustin froze. "I thought you just said I was getting you a bottle of water."

Michael cocked his head to one side. Disbelief filled his features. For a moment, he stared at Dustin in silence, confusing Dustin. Then he set his water aside. "Sorry. I have to know. I'll make you forget, but I have to know." He grabbed a knife from the butcher's block, sending Dustin's heart racing. Dustin floundered while Michael pressed the knife into Dustin's hand and then used Dustin to slice open Michael's forearm.

"What the hell are you doing?"

Michael quickly wiped the blood away, and the wound healed while Dustin watched. Dustin's hands shook. A scream rose in his throat but refused to fall from his lips. A scar immediately formed.

Dustin's hands shook. "What are you?"

Michael stared at Dustin. His face was pale, and he looked every bit as shocked as Dustin, as if he hadn't been the one to magically heal. "It can't be."

"What can't it be?" Dustin asked, yelling the question in his complete panic.

"You're my mate."

Questions bounced around the walls of his brain before disappearing. Dustin couldn't cling to a single thought. Ghosts were one thing. This was something else. Michael had been in his dreams. Now he was here, magically healing. "What in the fuck is going on, Michael?"

Michael's hands shook as he reached for Dustin. "Just one second more and I swear I'll let you forget. I can't let you go unclaimed, though. This risk is too great." His eyes swirled with clouds, mesmerizing Dustin and calming him. He forgot to be scared and then why he had been frightened to begin with. Michael's mouth covered his and nothing mattered any longer. His body burned. Michael's hands and lips were everywhere. His mouth moved to Dustin's throat. A small pain—like being stung by a bee—distracted Dustin for a half a second, and then the ecstasy was back. He wanted this. All of this. He hadn't known himself before Michael. Now he couldn't imagine life without him. Dustin had never felt so much so quickly. He should be terrified, but he wasn't. Then it was over.

Michael's lips lightly brushed his before pulling away. "You're such a temptation, but I promised you we'd get your fish tonight."

Dustin blinked. A tangy copper taste lingered on his tongue along with something sweet. It was almost like he had eaten blood covered cotton candy. Oddly, Dustin wanted to cling to the flavor forever. He set his water bottle aside.

"Fish. Right. Weren't we going to dinner too?"

Michael's mouth lifted in one corner in the sexiest smirk Dustin had ever seen. "We have a full night ahead of us."

The promise in Michael's voice couldn't be missed. Dustin wanted to be nervous, but he wasn't. It made no sense, but Dustin felt like he had been waiting his whole life for Michael. He couldn't back down now.

MICHAEL HAD EXCHANGED BLOOD WITH HIS mate in the shadiest way possible. He had zero regrets. After a lifetime of mistakes and chastisement from Celeste, she had chosen him a human mate. Michael wanted him. He wouldn't let Dustin deny him. Michael could explain his world later. Now Dustin needed his protection. Michael needed their blood tie. An angel mate would be in constant danger. Michael wouldn't risk the blessing he had been bestowed. If anything happened to Dustin, Michael needed to get to him as quickly as possible. That meant drinking each other's blood.

Even knowing he had been given the greatest gift he could ever imagine, Michael wasn't one hundred percent certain his exile had been lifted. He was taking a risk. If he got to the edge of his confinement area and couldn't leave, he would be forced to change Dustin's memories twice in one day. Michael really didn't want to do that. Still, he couldn't stop smiling. A human mate. Wow. He never dreamed.

A tightness hit him in the chest. His eyes burned. Michael hadn't spoken to Celeste in more years than he could count. He had never been angrier with anyone in his life than he had her. Michael understood his punishment. He recognized he was broken, but his ostracism had been cruel. Michael hadn't seen another soul in decades. Not since the last time a being had stumbled into his midst. Now he had a mate. It was so hard to believe that Michael questioned his sanity for half a second. Fear froze his feet to the ground halfway to Dustin's truck. What if it was an illusion? What if his mind had finally snapped and created a mate that didn't exist? His sanity couldn't withstand the loss.

Dustin stroked his arm. "Are you okay?"

Michael came back to himself. Dustin was real. He was really there. Michael would never be alone again. He fought a wave of tears. To hide his overwhelming emotions, Michael hauled Dustin against him and claimed his mouth once more. He was real. Thank the goddess.

I'll never abandon you.

Celeste's voice carried on the wind and caressed his hair. Michael barely held himself together. He stroked Dustin's cheek. Michael would cherish this gift for all of eternity. He couldn't be happier, even if he learned he was still banished.

When Michael finally let Dustin get some air, Dustin visibly fought a smile and kept sneaking glances Michael's way as they climbed inside the truck. Michael bit back a possessive growl. Dustin was young and innocent compared to Michael. Michael would have to teach him so many things. He couldn't wait. He got the feeling he would have to, though. As Dustin had pointed out several times, Dustin had never been with a man. This would be a different life for him. Dustin couldn't fight their blood tie. His fate. But he would likely try, and Michael had to be prepared for that.

As they neared the edge of Michael's set boundaries, his muscles tensed. He knew Celeste's wrath. Her memory could be long. His skin tingled. Michael held his breath. They crossed the line and nothing happened. Still, Michael's heart raced. Then reality set in. He was free. Tears sprang to Michael's eyes. He turned his head and stared out the passenger side window. Michael blindly reached for the Dustin's hand. He was pleasantly surprised when Dustin linked fingers with him. Dustin had set him free. He had a mate. Michael had given up hope of being worthy of such a blessing more years ago than he could count. He was supposed to be above the need for another half. Michael had honestly believed his exile was for eternity. Michael had accepted long ago that he was fractured in some way. He was a broken angel, because he needed love. That craving meant he had to stay locked away. Now he would have the love he longed for all these years. The knowledge was overwhelming.

"Any thoughts on where you'd like to eat?"

A slight panic overwhelmed Michael at the question. Not only didn't he eat, but Michael also knew very little about the current New Orleans. All the info he had about the world and New Orleans nowadays had been learned through the dreams of others. That wouldn't help him in this decision.

"I like everything," Michael said, hoping he could fake it. "Let's hit your favorite restaurant this time and I'll pick next time."

Dustin smiled. "Gumbo it is."

A wave of relief washed over Michael. He would have to spend Dustin's sleeping hours studying the town. For now, he couldn't stop watching Dustin. He was perfect.

"How long have you lived in New Orleans?"

At Dustin's question, Michael forced himself to stop picturing Dustin naked. It was only fair for him to let Dustin get to know him. "About five years."

Dustin nodded. "I know you were in the military before that. Where all have you lived?"

A smile tugged at Michael's lips. He couldn't be honest, but neither would he lie. Michael could hit the current highlights. "Before New Orleans, I spent a few years in Ireland and then New York. Before Ireland, Sweden." He saw Dustin picturing New York City in his head. Michael didn't bother correcting him. Celeste would have never confined him someplace with people. He had been on a farm. Celeste had moved him from town to town. Country to country. After New York, she never let him stay too close to people for long. She had made that mistake once. Celeste knew Michael could charm people to come to him through their dreams. He regretted nothing.

Michael shook off the memories that haunted him despite his defiant pride. "Do you like to travel?" Michael already knew the answer. He had seen Dustin's dreams.

A bright smile lit Dustin's features. "I'd like to think so, but I haven't gotten to go many places. At one time, I had an entire bucket list of places I wanted to see when I retired." Dustin shrugged. "Then I had to choose between continuing to work a job that slowly killed my soul or moving here. Obviously, I chose here. I don't regret anything, but that means giving up my dream of seeing the world. I have enough money to stay retired, but not enough to also travel the world."

"I'll take you to see the world."

A blush tinged Dustin's cheeks, fascinating Michael. He couldn't stop studying Dustin's every reaction. "Don't laugh, but—in a way—you already have. I dreamed about you."

Michael hummed. Even to his ears, he could tell the sound came out sexual as hell. "A dream. Tell me everything."

Dustin's blush deepened. "It was nothing, really. You had wings and flew me around the world, showing me all the places I want to see. It was... nice. I didn't want to wake up."

"Hold on to that feeling. I can make that dream come true."

Dustin glanced Michael's way at the claim. "You really sound like you could."

Dustin had no idea. Michael intended to show him things Dustin had never even imagined. The world was only the beginning. Dustin belonged to Michael now. They could visit any realm.

"You'll be happy with me." Even Michael heard the power in his vow. They were tied together for eternity now. Michael would give Dustin a beautiful life. He just needed time to prove it.

FOUR

YOU'LL BE happy with me. Those words ran through Dustin's mind all throughout dinner and buying fish. As they acclimated the koi to their new home, Dustin kept casting longing looks Michael's way. Michael really spoke like they were a couple after just a few kisses. Damned if Dustin didn't feel like it was true. He couldn't stop holding Michael's hand and stealing touches. Every time Michael's skin brushed his, it was like Dustin's heart sang. It sounded crazy, even to him, but he felt whole in some way he never had. No one understood. All his life, Dustin had felt like something was missing. As a child, he thought maybe he just hated being a kid. Then he had gone to college, and Dustin wondered if he just longed for a spouse. After he married,

Dustin thought maybe he needed to be free of a job to travel. There was always this itch in his soul for something more he couldn't find. Dustin's gaze moved Michael's way. He didn't feel that way now. He was at peace. Damn. Dustin saw it all now, and the truth was unexpected as hell. He was gay. How had he not known that? He was certain he had never looked at another man one single time and wanted him sexually. Then Michael had appeared and everything, yet nothing, made sense. Dustin wanted this.

Michael glanced his way and caught Dustin staring. His eyes flashed with mischief. "I thought the whole point in setting up this pond was to give you something peaceful to watch. Instead, you're staring at me."

Dustin fought a blush. "I'll get all Zen out here tomorrow. Right now, I'm tired as hell. This was hard work. I'm not sure I could've done it without you. At least, not in one day."

"It's my job to make your life easier."

Michael said the oddest things.

Dustin liked it. "It's not, but I appreciate you nonetheless."

The space between them got smaller as Michael shuffled closer. "We should shower, don't you think?"

Dustin glanced down at himself. He had done a lot of sweating today. Michael looked barely ruffled. It wasn't fair. "Yeah, I imagine I don't smell very good right now. I'm surprised they let us eat inside at the Crawfish Daddy. Can I see you tomorrow?"

Michael's smile looked a hell of a lot like he laughed at Dustin inside his head. "I meant we should shower together."

"Oh." Dustin didn't know if he should cover his face in embarrassment or run for the hills. He shifted from foot to foot. The immediate nervousness had him nearly crawling from his skin. "I'm not sure I'm ready for that." He wanted to be. God knew his body was on fire, but damn. He knew fuck all about dating a man. Michael might want things Dustin didn't know if he could do. Yet there was a hunger in Dustin's gut he hadn't expected. He suddenly wanted everything. Images of being on his knees flashed through Dustin's head. Scene after scene flared in his imagination. He wanted to sit on Michael's face and taste Michael's cock. Dustin longed for Michael's dick to fill his ass. He didn't know where this came from. Dustin wasn't ready. He needed to think.

Michael's body collided with his and Dustin realized he was rock hard and there was no way Michael couldn't feel the erection stabbing him. His blue gaze looked incredibly kind and understanding. "It's okay, baby. I want you, but I can wait until you're ready."

There was a voice inside Dustin's head, screaming he wanted to get dicked down right there in the yard. His mouth had other plans. "Thank you. I want this. I want you, but I'm also trying not to freak out. This came out of nowhere, but I'm happy it did." Dustin knew he did a piss-poor job of explaining his thoughts. He was thrilled to be here with Michael. Dustin was just a little overwhelmed.

You'll always be safe with me.

"I'm sure that's true, but I just need a little more time."

Michael's bright smile made Dustin wonder what he had said that made Michael so happy. Thankfully,

Michael cleared things up before Dustin over thought things. "I'm proud as hell of you. You could've pretended there's no spark between us and shut me down immediately. I get how lucky I am to have met you."

Dustin thought he might explode with happiness. His heart had never felt so full. He found his hands moving of their own accord, caressing Michael's chest and drawing him closer. His mouth went dry at the heat that flared in Michael's expression. Dustin couldn't let him get away just yet. "Before you go, maybe one last kiss."

The words barely left Dustin's lips before Michael's mouth covered his. Their tongues stroked and battled. Michael was every bit as hard for Dustin as Dustin was for him. All hints of embarrassment fled. Dustin was turned on and floating on cloud nine.

By the time Michael pulled away, Dustin was panting. Michael walked backward. "Tomorrow."

Dustin nodded. "I can't wait."

For a few more seconds, Michael kept walking backward before turning away. The second he did, Dustin touched his lips. Wow. He felt overwhelmed and ecstatic. Happiness filled him to overflowing. He fought the urge to chase after Michael and beg him to come back. Instead, he headed inside and locked the door behind him. Exhaustion weighed heavily on his limbs. Dustin went straight to the bathroom to shower. He didn't have the energy for anything else. While waiting for the water to heat, Dustin stood beside the glass shower door and stripped. The full-length mirror across from the shower caught his gaze. He swore he looked different today. Younger. It didn't make sense. Something about his infatuation with Michael made Dustin feel at least ten years younger. His knees no longer hurt. It was as if Michael healed something inside him he hadn't known was broken. He couldn't recall ever feeling so much so fast. It was like no one else existed.

Dustin stepped inside the shower and the hot water and steam engulfed him. He tilted his chin up and wet his hair. An image flared to life behind his closed lids. Michael's lips touched Dustin's throat. His nude body pressed against Dustin's. Their erections bumped. Dustin's breath caught. His body was on fire. Inside his head, Michael kissed his way down Dustin's body while dropping to his knees. Dustin palmed his cock and stroked. It wasn't the same as

Michael's hot mouth, but Michael sucked Dustin in Dustin's fantasy. Dustin had never been more turned on. He knew how best to please himself. His hips rolled. He fucked his fist with Michael's name on his lips. Dustin didn't drag things out. He needed to blow with Michael's name on his tongue. His knees nearly gave out as his orgasm hit. For a split second, it was almost like Michael was really there. Dustin swore he could smell him. Then the moment was gone, and Dustin was left panting and shaking. He finished his shower in a haze of hunger. Tomorrow couldn't get here soon enough. He needed more of Michael.

As Dustin stepped from the shower, his mind froze, and his skin turned to ice. A full fresh handprint cut through the fog coating the full-length mirror across from the shower. It was too recent for the steam to have time to fill in the print and too large to be from Dustin's hand. It was exactly as if someone had braced their weight on their palm on the mirror only seconds earlier. He wasn't alone.

Dustin grabbed his towel and wrapped it around his waist as he crept from the bathroom. He checked around each corner before slipping inside his bedroom. The loaded shotgun behind his door was still there. Once Dustin had it held high, he cleared every room, checking the closets, behind doors, and under beds. By the time he was finished, every inch of the place had been scoured. He couldn't do this anymore. His insides shook. There was something inside his home. Dustin could no longer pretend ignorance. There was a real chance he wasn't safe.

After throwing on some clothes, Dustin found his cellphone and searched the name of the voodoo shop Michael mentioned. According to their website, they closed in thirty minutes. There was no way Dustin could make it in time. He dialed the number before he talked himself out of doing so.

His call was answered on the third ring. "This is Baptiste."

That was good. He needed someone in charge. "Hi. A friend of mine suggested your shop to me, but I live out in the bayou and there's no way I can get there in time. Is there any way you can wait for me? I have an emergency."

"What type of emergency?"

At least they weren't hanging up on him. "I think there's something in my house. It sounds crazy, I know, but I'm not alone. I think I need some help."

"Do you feel you're in danger from this entity?"

Dustin blew out a breath. "I don't know. Possibly."

"Okay. Head our way and I'll wait. If you're not here by closing, just knock. I'll be here."

"Thank you. I'll hurry." Dustin disconnected and rushed to find his shoes. He appreciated Baptiste being willing to wait. There was something going on, and Dustin needed to know what. He didn't want to live in fear in his own home. His brain skirted away from what he had been doing in the shower while he had been spied upon by god only knew what.

He drove to the Quarter with his heart in his throat. There was still a small part of him that wanted to revert to thinking he was crazy or misremembering. The only thing that stopped him from turning around was knowing some poor guy waited after closing time to help him.

By the time he made it to Baptiste's Voodoo Shoppe, the place was mostly dark. There was only a small light coming from the back of the store. Dustin knocked, half hoping his knock went unanswered. If so, then he could go back to pretending nothing happened. Unfortunately, he didn't get the chance to consider that option for long. A shadow moved toward the door. The door opened and Dustin found himself staring at a much younger man than he expected. They were possibly close to the same age. The guy might be a little younger. His dark blond hair was short cropped. It didn't have a hint of gray. Something about him immediately put Dustin at ease.

For a moment, Dustin forgot to introduce himself. He almost felt like Baptiste already knew. "Hi. I'm Dustin. We spoke on the phone."

Baptiste took a step back, letting Dustin inside. "Hey, Dustin. I'm Baptiste. Tell me what's been going on?"

Dustin moved inside and started at the beginning. "I recently moved into my grandparents' historic home. Almost immediately, I started noticing things out of place. Things weren't where I left them. That sort of thing. Then tonight, when I got out of the shower, there was a fresh handprint on the steamed over mirror. It wasn't mine and I live alone. I'm a pretty big nonbeliever of the paranormal, but there is something or someone in my house."

Baptiste nodded. "Without checking your house personally, I don't know what to give you for protection. Would you be open to me calling a friend? He's somewhat of a psychic. He can see whatever you've seen. He's right out back. I can have him here in a matter of seconds."

Dustin nodded. He was so relieved Baptiste didn't think he was insane that he would agree to anything. "Yeah. Whatever you need."

Baptiste motioned for him to wait. He headed for the back of the shop and immediately returned with another man in tow. This man's long dark hair and light blue eyes held Dustin captive. When he spoke, Dustin was reminded of a pirate. "I'm Dante. Baptiste filled me in. Is it okay if touch you so I can see your memories?"

In truth, Dustin really didn't want that. He didn't think he could say no, since he had come to them for help. "I guess."

With a short nod, Dante set his hand on Dustin's forearm. His expression went from impersonal to baffled in an instant. He glanced behind him and motioned Baptiste closer. "Did you see?"

Baptiste nodded. "That's why I called you. Change his eye color and he could be someone else."

Dante looked taken aback. "I was thinking change his hair color."

Both men looked Dustin's way. "Who is your mate?"

Dustin blinked. "What?"

"Your mate. Who is he?"

Confusion had Dustin tripping over his words. "I don't... what do you mean? I came here about a haunting. What are you talking about?"

"We should take him to King Jonathan."

Dante grabbed Dustin's arm. A shot of fear hit Dustin in the chest. Before he could protest, he stood in the middle of an unfamiliar road in the middle of nowhere.

"We'll have to walk from here."

Dustin fought not hyperventilate. He tried pulling out of Dante's hold, but the man was too strong. "Get your hands off—" A bright flash of light exploded, lighting up the night sky. Dante was ripped away from Dustin. Dustin's ass hit the ground. Huge white wings blocked Dustin from seeing what became of Dante.

A roar rent the air. "How dare you touch my mate?"

An odd sense of peace overcame Dustin as one wing shifted, and Michael glanced over his shoulder. "Are you okay, baby?"

Dustin nodded and scrambled to his feet. There was a small part of him that realized he should be completely freaked out. It was possible he was in shock. In Dustin's heart, he knew the truth. He had always known Michael was really the angel from his dreams. His dreams had been too real. It was crazy. But then again, so had everything been since his move. Michael was the good type of insanity. Dustin glanced past Michael as he came to his feet. Dante was on his knees with his head bowed.

Giant men in kilts appeared from the darkness. One by one, they hit their knees at the sight of Michael. Dustin couldn't tell if it happened willingly. Michael seemed to be too worried about Dustin's well-being to explain what was happening. Dustin fought hard to keep the panic at bay.

"What is going on?"

Michael stroked his cheek. "I have a feeling you're about to meet my sons."

Oddly, that was the most terrifying thought all night.

POOR DUSTIN LOOKED SHELLSHOCKED. AS HE should. Michael had planned to ease Dustin into his new reality. There was no going back from here. He had juggled the idea of wiping Dustin's memory again. The idea died a swift death at Dustin's reaction to Michael in full archangel glory. He didn't flinch away. In fact, he didn't even look surprised. Dustin seemed more horrified by his treatment from the vampire. Michael was still considering that one's fate. Michael answered to no one but Celeste. In the hierarchy, he was one step below a god. Archangels were the pure blood children and grandchildren of deities. Michael was one of the oldest. He did not appreciate the treatment of his mate.

Michael held his arm out. He was beyond pleased

when Dustin didn't hesitate to let Michael tuck him against his side. He even held tight to Michael's waist, openly seeking Michael's refuge. A smile tugged at Michael's lips as he stared into his mate's eyes. Dustin's thoughts were all over the place, but his fear for Michael was real. Dustin cared more about Michael's wellbeing than his own, even though he was the only one there who could die. He should have known Celeste would pick a mate for him strong enough to stand at his side through anything. Dustin hadn't let him down. In fact, Dustin was proud to have his dream angel at his side. Everything about being with Dustin was humbling.

"Are you sure you're okay?"

Dustin nodded. "I'm just really confused and..." Dustin didn't seem to know how to finish.

Michael understood. He whisked his lips across Dustin's. "I'll explain everything soon. Right now, this vampire has some explaining to do."

"Vampire?" Dustin choked on the question.

Explanations would have to wait. Michael turned a cold stare Dante's way, but he didn't miss the way Dustin clung tighter to him. "Explain yourself."

Dante didn't lift his eyes. "I'm sorry, your grace. When I looked inside your mate's mind, I thought he might be in danger from a demon or unknown shifter. You look so much like—"

A flash of light cut through the darkness, cutting short Dante's explanation. "Why are my men on their knees? They don't serve..." Jonathan's words died as he focused on Michael.

One of the kilted warriors did a poor job of whispering. "It's an archangel, Jonathan. He must be treated as if we're standing before Celeste herself."

Jonathan seemed unfazed by the info. Considering he was Celeste's grandson, Michael got it. Jonathan would bow to no one. "Why do you look so much like..." Jonathan shook his head. "Please come inside. I swear your mate will be safe and treated with the highest respect."

Michael's gaze moved to Dante. His anger still simmered. He knew it showed in his features. Michael couldn't control it. His thoughts were proven correct when Jonathan stepped forward and touched Dante's shoulder. He not only disappeared, but his whereabouts were hidden from Michael. It was obvious Jonathan wouldn't allow Michael to punish Dante.

Jonathan motioned toward the iron gates behind him. "Please."

Michael wrapped a wing around Dustin as he pulled him tighter into his embrace, protecting him as they fell into step behind Jonathan. His wings were impenetrable. No harm would come to Michael's heart.

Dustin shook to his core.

Michael hated that.

"Why are his wings black?" Dustin whispered as they made their way up the driveway. "Is he a demon?"

Wolves surrounded them the second they breached the property line. Michael's skin glowed as he doubled his protection around Dustin. Wolves didn't serve Celeste. He didn't think they would bow to him.

Jonathan flashed a smile over his shoulder, obviously hearing Dustin's question. "I'm not a demon. Even though that wouldn't make me inherently bad, I'm a

Nephilim and the vampire king. My name is Jonathan." He motioned toward the closest kilted warrior. "This is my mate, or husband, as you would know him, Niall." He motioned to another warrior on his other side. "This is my other mate, Cin." He waved toward the three warriors following them. "Those three are Faolan, Dougal, and Lire. There are others inside, but this is our clan. The Hellish from Scotland."

Michael could hear Dustin's thoughts racing. His fear and confusion beat at Michael's brain. Michael kept Dustin's thoughts hidden from the beasts surrounding them. He didn't want them knowing Dustin mulled over everyone calling him Michael's mate, or husband, as Jonathan had pointed out. Part of Dustin thought he was dreaming. Michael had too much to handle at once.

"What brings an archangel to New Orleans?"

Michael definitely didn't want to have that conversation, but he also recognized it couldn't be avoided. "This is where my sons are."

"You still haven't introduced yourself," Jonathan pointed out as he led them inside a huge mansion that was oddly homelike.

Michael stroked Dustin, seeking comfort from his mate. "I am the archangel, Michael."

Jonathan missed a step as he spun Michael's way.

Everyone froze, eyeing everyone else.

Michael shifted his focus Dustin's way. Dustin looked exhausted and terrified. He had been overwhelmed for the night and Michael couldn't force anymore on him. His heart twisted at the dark circles beneath Dustin's eyes. He knew they were his fault. While holding Dustin's stare, he spoke to Jonathan. "My mate is human. He doesn't keep to vampire hours, and he's had a rough night. Is there somewhere he can rest?"

A blond sprite appeared behind the demon Lire, as if he had been there the whole time. using the demon as a living shield. "He can stay with me. I'd keep him safe."

Michael's throat swelled as he looked at the blue eyes that matched his. He fought to control his voice as he spoke. "I know you would, but I would very much like for you to stay."

"Oh, boy," Jonathan muttered. "We have to find Dustin a room fast because shit is getting real around here."

A smile pulled at Michael's lips. Despite everything, he had never been filled with so much hope. There was so much about this day he never expected.

"Oh. Okay." Tam sounded incredibly sweet. "Evan could stay with your mate, then. If that's okay? He's my best friend and really nice, but also an amazing protector. He's the wolf companion of a god's mate. Appointed by Odin and everything."

Michael gave a small nod. "If Odin has vouched for his honor, I will allow him to protect my mate." He looked Dustin's way. "Is that okay, baby?"

Dustin nodded. "I'll be fine."

Michael had never known this much pride.

A brown-haired and blue-eyed boy who looked to be no older than twenty stepped inside the room. He boldly held Michael's stare, looking unafraid. Yet Michael could feel his kindness. He possessed a blindingly pure soul. The boy dipped his chin. "I'm Evan. Dustin will be safe with me."

If you get scared, just call out in your mind. I can hear you and nothing will stop me from coming to you.

At Michael's mental blast, Dustin held his gaze and nodded. Michael almost abandoned this mess right then. Dustin needed him right now. Everyone else there was merely curious about him. Dustin was the only one who wouldn't survive without him.

Evan led Dustin away. Michael watched him go with his heart in his throat.

"I swear to you he will be safe in my home," Jonathan said, reassuring Michael. "You have my word. My clan will not allow anything to happen to him."

Michael couldn't stop himself from explaining the moment Dustin was out of earshot. "He doesn't understand. Your people terrified him."

Jonathan nodded. "I'm sorry about that. Dante didn't know our world hadn't been explained to your mate."

Despite his best efforts, Michael's temper flared. "No. He didn't care my mate doesn't understand. He simply used his powers to take Dustin without his permission because he could. That's not right. It's not honorable." Michael was angrier than he realized now that some of the adrenaline had worn off. "You claim your clan will keep him safe, yet your people took him in the first place. King or not, you'll never rule me, and it's not your right to accost the mate of an archangel."

"Are you Jonathan's dad?"

Tam's quiet question cut through Michael's rage. His gaze shot the tiny blond's way. As Michael's gaze landed upon him, Tam half hid behind his demon friend. He twisted a doll, as if nervous to have Michael's attention, but his gaze never wavered from Michael.

Michael's throat swelled.

Tam didn't give up. "It's just that, except for your eyes and wings, you two look exactly alike, and Celeste is Jonathan's grandmother. Since you're... I just thought..." He twisted the doll some more.

Michael swallowed past the lump in his throat. "Actually, I have two children."

"Oh." Tam scratched the bridge of his nose and shifted from foot to foot. "I can't read your mind. I can read everyone's mind, but not you."

A smile tugged at Michael's lips. "I'm very old and very powerful."

"Maybe we should all sit," Niall suggested.

Michael blinked. He needed to keep his wits. Just because he loved his sons, that didn't mean they would love him back. Likely, they hadn't known he existed. His chest hurt. They had been kept apart for so long. "Yes. Perhaps we should."

As a unit, they moved farther into the sitting room. Michael chose a seat where his back would be in the corner so he could see all attackers.

Tam and Jonathan sat together on a loveseat flanked by mates and guards. It was obvious Michael was the outsider. No matter his position, they would fight to the death to protect their king.

"I've been exiled," Michael said, not knowing where else to start. "That's why you thought I was dead."

Jonathan gave a jerky nod, proving he already knew the truth in his heart.

Tam looked fascinated. "Why were you exiled?"

"Because I fathered you."

Tam laughed. When no one else did, his smile died away. A small line appeared between his eyebrows. He twisted his doll. "My parents were a shifter and a mage. You're an angel."

Michael took a deep breath. He didn't know how to explain. "Many years ago, I had another son who was stillborn. Celeste was furious and banished me to the woods of Sweden. When your mother wandered into my forest, I was half mad after a millennium alone. When she realized she carried my child, I panicked and tried strengthening your blood with magic. I knew Celeste would be angry, but I couldn't risk watching another child die. Celeste plucked me from the forest and dropped me on a two-hundred-acre farm in New York. I raged at missing your birth, and then your mother passed, and you disappeared. I couldn't be consoled. Then a female human found me. She spent two years putting me back together." His gaze shifted Jonathan's way. "Jonathan was born seemingly completely human. Yet Celeste still swept me away to Ireland. When she dropped me here about five years ago, I didn't understand why I had been moved again until I felt you. I've been trapped in the bayou ever since." He shook his head. "I thought she kept me close to you to punish me even more. I never thought she'd let me see you."

Everyone stared at him in silence.

Tam seemed to be the only one who was either too forgiving, too curious, or too confused to be angry. "But I'm almost ten years younger than Jonathan. Your story doesn't make sense."

A smile tugged at Michael's lips. "Jonathan was born human and grew into his powers. He'll age differently. You're nearly a century older than him."

Tam shook his head. Michael could feel him getting more upset by the second. He rocked himself. "No. I'm younger. I can't be your son."

Tam's mate dropped to his haunches at Tam's feet, openly trying to console him. "Sweetie, time moves differently in Hell. For all we know, you might have stopped aging there and started again once you were free. We just can't know."

Tam shook his head. "He can't be my dad. If he's my dad, then Celeste is my grandmother too, and she hates me. She would never accept that. I can't... I just can't."

Michael's eyes burned. His throat ached. For more years than he could count, Michael had dreamed of meeting his sons. Now his worst fears were coming true. They hated him for the same reasons Celeste had exiled him. He was the broken angel.

He stood. "I should take my mate home." For a moment, he stared at nothing, wishing he could say something to fix everything. There was nothing powerful enough to explain how he had suffered. He didn't meet anyone's gaze. "Every day, I wished to be with you. I've raged at my circumstances and been more insane than not for longer than I can recall. I'm sorry your lives were not what you deserved because of me. My only solace is that you have each other. It's okay if you need to pretend my story is a lie."

With his heart in his throat, Michael followed the thrum of his mate's life force. He wished they hadn't taken Dustin and left him no choice but to show himself. Michael had known his sons were better off without him. Now it was too late to take it all back.

FIVE

THE ROOM HAD CLEARED ALMOST INSTANTLY the moment Michael left, leaving Jonathan alone with Tam. Jonathan could feel the hurt and confusion rolling off Tam in waves. For Jonathan, learning Tam's father was an archangel who had toyed with Tam's blood in the womb explained so much. He had always known Tam was incredibly powerful for reasons they couldn't explain. Still, Jonathan felt somewhat at sea. He felt like something really important had been stolen from him. His first instinct was to head straight to Celeste and demand answers. He couldn't leave Tam.

Jonathan took Tam's hand. The moment their fingers linked, Tam's grip tightened. He cast a nervous glance Jonathan's way. "I love you."

Jonathan's heart warmed. "I love you too."

A tear rolled down Tam's cheek. "This can't be true."

"Why not?" Jonathan truly didn't understand why Tam was so adamant.

Tam's expression crumbled as he slid further into despair. "Because Celeste would hate that."

"That's not true."

Jonathan blinked at their surroundings. They still sat on a loveseat, but they were surrounded by light and beauty. Tiny teacups sat on the white coffee table, and Celeste sat across from them. They had been transported to the heavens.

"That's not true," Celeste repeated, sounding upset.

Tam moved so quickly, Jonathan had no hope of not having his wings damaged. He snapped to fox form and skittered behind Jonathan, hiding between Jonathan's back and wings.

Celeste stood and claimed the now empty spot at Jonathan's side. Her blonde curls were perfect as always, and her green eyes were filled with tears. She easily plucked Tam from behind Jonathan's back. Tam went limp, pretending to be dead as she set him in her lap. Celeste stroked his fur, openly trying to soothe him.

"Sweet angel. I have loved you all your life. You have no idea how it broke me when you went missing. I cannot see into Hell. It's not my realm. All I could do was wait for Jonathan to come into his powers and hope he could find you."

"Why did you keep Michael from us?"

Jonathan didn't want to be angry. He loved and trusted Celeste. This was one time he didn't understand. Their lives could have been different. They could have had each other.

Celeste held his stare. He couldn't miss her certainty when she spoke. "Neither of you would be who you are if you were raised by your father. My angels are all powerful and have been since the day they were born. You cannot understand the arrogance or the suffering that comes with that responsibility. They can have whatever they want whenever they want, but then again, they can have nothing. Can you imagine if all my children and grandchildren littered the world with Nephilim? You are good and kind, but that isn't true of all creatures. I'm not even sure it's true of most. Michael has always been... different." Celeste winced as she made the confession, as if it pained her. "Most angels are stoic in their loneliness, or they stay here in the heavens where there is peace. Michael loved the world too much to leave. He loves everything about humans and life. It's a fire in his blood. He had too many years to wait for his true mate to be born. Life has been too long for him. He has felt every second of his existence tick by while he waited for Dustin. I'm sorry my decisions have hurt you both. It's not easy being all-knowing. I can see what you cannot. Each tiny change in birth and circumstance transforms the character of every person. You are both so important to keeping the balance of the world. I had no choice."

Tears spilled over Celeste's lashes as she looked down at Tam. "I'm so sorry, Tamil. I don't stay away because I hate you. I stay away because you should hate me."

Tam became human again.

Jonathan fought a ridiculous urge to laugh.

If Tam wasn't tiny and Celeste wasn't a god, she would have been squashed beneath his sudden transformation. Instead, she held him like a large child. They stared at each other with so much love that Jonathan's heart ached to be a part of it. Tam needed it more than Jonathan did.

Celeste reached over and took Jonathan's hand. Her gaze moved between them. "Michael has his mate now. With Dustin at his side, Michael is free again. His hurt, anger, and guilt will likely keep him away from you. He thinks you hate him and blame him for his absence. I know him too well. He won't reach out. Just as I've been too stubborn to reach for Tam."

"It's not your fault," Tam said, making Jonathan proud. "Everyone is scared of something."

Celeste cried harder. "You two are my greatest creations. No one makes me prouder."

Jonathan's gaze moved to Tam. They met each other's stare. The truth of their crazy night washed over Jonathan in a powerful wave of emotion. They were brothers. He never dreamed he could be so blessed.

THE SCENT OF COTTON CANDY FILLED DUSTIN'S nose. He inhaled. His eyes opened. Soft, white feathers engulfed him from head to toe. Dustin had never been more comfortable in his life. He was nude and, in his bed, the way he slept each night. Dustin didn't remember going to bed or falling asleep. Part of him wanted to think everything had been a dream. But there was no denying there was a giant wing blanketing him.

Dustin stroked the feathers. He couldn't stop himself. They felt and smelled amazing. They stirred, coming to life beneath his touch. Dustin turned his head. Michael's sexy face was inches from his. As Dustin looked on, Michael's full lips parted on a pant, but his eyes didn't open. Dustin stroked the wing again.

"Shit." Michael dragged out the curse in a sexy, low growl that immediately hardened Dustin's cock. He wondered what it said about him that he wasn't freaking out at all.

"It's because you've always known me," Michael said. His voice was deeper, heavy with sleep. One blue eye opened. "You've felt me in the back of your mind your entire life." His arm shot out and curled around Dustin, pulling him deeper into his embrace. It felt like they were in their own little bubble, cocooned away from the rest of the world beneath Michael's wing. He didn't have to fear anything here.

Dustin mulled over Michael's claim. It was true. His entire life, something had been pulling him in a different direction from the life he had been living. He saw it now. Something had been drawing him to Michael. Another thought hit. "You can hear my thoughts."

Michael nodded. "And you can hear mine."

Dustin soaked that in. It was true. There were times he heard Michael in his head.

Michael's hand slid down Dustin's body. *Tell me to stop.*

No.

After everything that happened last night, all that he had discovered about the world, suddenly, making love to a man seemed like nothing to fear. Michael's palm smoothed over Dustin's erection, cupping him.

Dustin's eyes fell closed. Pleasure made his eyelids too heavy to keep open.

Why do I feel so much?

Michael rolled and pinned Dustin to the bed at his mental question. "There's so much this body can do you haven't explored."

Dustin's eyes opened. He shook his head as he stared up at Michael. "I meant in my heart. Why do I feel so much? I was married for twelve years and never felt this much."

"Because you're mine," Michael growled, making Dustin's cock leak. "You are the other half of me. This is more than love. It's cosmic. We were written in the stars."

Before Dustin could lose himself in the million questions he had, Michael claimed his lips. Their kiss rocked Dustin's soul. He kissed an angel. Dustin was acutely aware of that fact. It was mind blowing.

Michael moved lower, kissing Dustin's neck. "You haven't seen mind blowing yet."

Dustin gasped for air as Michael moved lower. He wasn't sure how he felt about Michael hearing his every thought, but he couldn't care at the moment. Michael's teeth scraped Dustin's nipple as he kissed a path down Dustin's body. The moment he almost begged, Michael's hot mouth sucked Dustin's dick. Dustin's hips left the bed, seeking more. His mind was a complete mess. All Dustin could do was feel and cling to the headboard. Saliva rolled down his length. The blow job was sloppy and perfect. Michael was in control. Tight suction had Dustin locked in ecstasy. Then two fingers stretched his asshole. Dustin spread his thighs like a wanton, begging for more. Michael finger-fucked Dustin's asshole, hitting a spot Dustin didn't know existed. Noises escaped Dustin he had never made in his life. He writhed like a whore. Dustin had never felt more sexual. He was pure desire and need. Dustin was out of his head. He rolled his hips, fucking Michael's throat while grinding down on Michael's fingers, wanting everything. Pressure beat at his crown. He whimpered, fighting for release. Even when the explosion came, Dustin didn't soften. His need didn't lessen. He had to have more.

"Fuck me," Dustin begged, sounding inhuman even to his ears. Nothing existed beyond his lust for more. When Michael shot upward and impaled Dustin with his dick, there was no pain. Dustin's mind was too far gone. Another orgasm had him shaking, and still his dick wouldn't go down. Even as cum poured from his cock, soaking his skin, Dustin wanted more. He had never felt greedier. Dustin needed to push his body to the edge. As long as Michael could keep this up, Dustin wanted it. No matter how much he hurt later.

"That's it, Dustin." Michael stared down at Dustin with an intensity Dustin had never seen. He was held captive by the power of it. "Take all of me." Until the words left Michael's lips, Dustin hadn't realized Michael still wasn't all the way in.

"I don't know if I can." He had already taken way more than he ever imagined he could.

Michael thrust, shoving even more dick inside Dustin. "You can." He thrust again, getting even deeper. "I'm going to make you fly."

At the promise, Dustin's muscles relaxed, and Michael drove to the hilt. Dustin's eyes rolled back as their souls seemed to connect. "Fuck." The word dragged from deep within Dustin. He doubted he would have enjoyed this with anyone else. Dustin recognized Michael kept the pain at bay.

Michael grabbed his chin, demanding Dustin's attention at the thought. "There is no one else. Not ever. You belong to me. This asshole. Your body. Your soul. They're all mine." Michael almost sounded demonic.

Dustin felt... whole—like he had waited his entire life to hear those words. "I'm yours."

At Dustin's agreement, Michael's eyes fell closed as if he savored the moment. He looked intoxicated by Dustin's words. Then his eyes opened, and Dustin knew he was about to get fucked. Michael's mouth slammed against his with enough force Dustin tasted blood. Their tongues fought while Michael pumped inside him. Skin slapped skin too fast for Dustin to keep up. All he could do was take it. He couldn't explain the sensations washing over him. Dustin had never felt like this. His soul sang. As the third orgasm built, so too did an odd need to bite. His teeth itched with it. Michael's mouth moved to Dustin's neck. Dustin stared at Michael's shoulder, incapable of resisting. He kissed the tanned, muscular skin exposed to his mouth. The moment his lips touched Michael's shoulder, something inside him snapped. He bit. Blood filled his mouth as light popped behind his eyes. The hardest orgasm he had ever experienced ripped through him. A sharp pain in his neck flared into ecstasy. Dustin swore his soul left his body while he shook in Michael's arms. Something tugged inside his chest, tying him to Michael.

"I love you." The words tore from Dustin's spirit. They felt realer than any words he had ever spoken. He had never known truth before Michael. This was where he had always belonged.

"I love you too."

Pure happiness exploded through him. He had found fate.

THEY WERE OFFICIALLY MATED IN EVERY WAY now. Michael couldn't tear his gaze away from Dustin. His hunger was nowhere near slated. He wanted to bathe in Dustin's cum. Michael's heart required he take care of Dustin's health. Even though Dustin would never die, Michael still needed to know Dustin felt his absolute best.

"What do you mean I'll never die?"

Michael winced. He had never had to hide his thoughts before Dustin. Not that he wanted to do so now, but he also didn't want to scare Dustin. He had to be honest, though. "You're an angel mate. That means your life is tied to mine. I cannot die, so neither will you."

Dustin chewed his bottom lip and stared at Michael. His mind was all over the place, making it hard for Michael to see his thoughts clearly. "Everyone keeps talking about mates and I don't really understand."

Michael nodded. He got that. "Celeste, she is who humans call God. She pairs each being with a soulmate. For humans, it's typically another human, and they'll find each other in every lifetime. For immortals, we only have the one eternal life. Our soulmates walk with us through the millennia. We will never die. Our love will only grow stronger. You will never crave anyone else sexually with the power you feel for me. Nothing or no one will ever be as important as we are to each other. It is the greatest of blessings to be gifted a true life mate."

Dustin nodded along. Michael could see he felt the truth in Michael's words. His questions became clearer in his mind. "Who is Celeste to you?"

"She is my grandmother. I am the only son of the original Michael. The one most humans know."

A line appeared between Dustin's eyebrows. "But one of your sons is the king of vampires."

Michael nodded. "The Americas pack, to be precise. A child born between a human and an angel is a Nephilim. He is the most powerful being in the universe. That's why I was exiled. Jonathan is pure of heart, but his existence is dangerous. Celeste couldn't allow me to have more children."

"But you have two."

"Tamil," Michael said in agreement. "His mother came to me in human form, but she was a shifter. Tam is every bit as powerful as Jonathan. Maybe even more so, but he is broken and scared of his powers. Thankfully, he too is pure of heart. I was very lucky I didn't cause the end of times. It's possible I'm not very good at being an angel."

"I think you're amazing."

Michael stared at Dustin with his heart in his throat. In many ways, they should be complete strangers, but they weren't. They had literally been made for each other. To Michael, Dustin was the most perfect creature ever created. It meant everything to him to have Dustin's favor.

"Everyone who ever overlooked you in life for any reason is the biggest fool in creation. I'm glad they were, though. Otherwise, you might not have found me."

Dustin shook his head. "I don't believe that. I think no matter what happened or where I was, I would've found you. Like you said, souls find each other in every life. I would've found you."

Michael buried his face in the crook of Dustin's neck and held on. He had been so isolated and on the verge of full-blown insanity for so long. Dustin would never understand how much he meant to Michael, but Michael would make him see. He would spend eternity spoiling his mate for all others. If it was the last thing he did, it wouldn't be only their bond holding them together. Dustin would see. He wouldn't regret this.

SIX

A WEEK PASSED in a passion-filled haze. They barely left their bed. Michael explained his world in between bouts of lovemaking. Dustin listened and tried not to freak too much. He had seen the creatures that lived in the dark firsthand. They were as real as him. He couldn't deny the world hidden behind a cloak of magic. Dustin lived there now.

As much as Dustin hated it, he had to do something other than bask in the light of his mate's love. He still had a garden to plant, a few boxes left to unpack, and some cleaning to do. It was a lot more fun with a nude Michael walking around the house. When a knock landed on the front door, Michael's wings disappeared, and clothes appeared in their place. It surprised Dustin how much he hated Michael hiding behind a human disguise. He wanted Michael to be free.

Dustin answered the door to a group of Scottish warriors and the tiny blond who had his father's eyes.

Tam waved. "Hi. Oh, I like your house." Tam turned into a fox and zipped past Dustin. Dustin watched in confused fascination as Tam zoomed around his house, sniffing of things before taking off again. He ran so fast, he made Dustin's head spin.

"You have to excuse Tam. *Someone* let him have coffee this morning." Dustin stared at Michael's other son in awe. Now that Dustin was rested and not scared for his life, he recognized how truly regal Jonathan looked. His black wings dragged on the ground, and he towered over Dustin by nearly a foot. He had eyes like leprechaun gold and fangs that should have scared Dustin but didn't. He was oddly soothing.

One of the Scots laughed. His amethyst eyes screamed good humor. "I thought it would be good for a laugh and I was right. The boy hasn't stopped spinning all morning."

Jonathan rolled his eyes.

Dustin realized he still had everyone standing on the porch. "Oh. Please come in."

With a nod, Jonathan stepped inside. "I don't know if you remember everyone, but I'm Jonathan." He motioned toward each person as they filed inside, reminding Dustin of their names. "Faolan, Dougal, Niall, Cin, and Tam's mate, Risk. I don't believe you met him."

A man with gorgeous dark skin nodded at Dustin. "It is nice to meet you."

Dustin smiled. "I'm Dustin. Feel free to sit anywhere." He glanced Michael's way. Michael still wore his human guise. He stood proudly with his hands clasped behind his back. Even though he looked hard, Dustin could feel his nervousness.

As the men filled the couch, loveseat, and recliner, Tam skittered to a stop an inch from Dustin and turned back into a man. He clasped his head as if it spun.

"Whoa. Everything is moving really fast."

Dustin chuckled. Faolan was right. It was a little funny. "Maybe you should drink some water."

Tam's nose wiggled. "I smell lemonade. Can I have lemonade?"

With a smile, Dustin led Tam to the fridge and fixed him a glass. Tam guzzled the drink. It didn't look like it helped much.

"You have fish outside. Can I go play with the fish?"

Dustin shrugged. "If you'd like. I don't know if fish really play or not, but you can try."

Tam nodded. "Don't worry. I can be a fish too and fish like other fish."

Risk stood and plucked Tam from his feet. "Come on, angel. It's time to sit and calm down. You'll get wet playing with the fish."

Tam settled down with Risk's arms wrapped around him. Risk carried Tam to the recliner and sat.

Dustin grabbed a chair from the kitchen table and carried it to the living room. He motioned for Michael to sit.

Michael shook his head. "You take that one. I'll grab one for myself."

Since Michael was already headed to grab another, Dustin sat. He smiled at their guests, feeling somewhat awkward. "Would anyone like something to drink?"

Everyone shook their heads and Dustin fell back into an uncomfortable silence.

Jonathan tried to make small talk. "Did you know we're neighbors? Your property backs against ours."

At Jonathan's claim, Dustin's gaze shot to Michael. "I thought your cabin backed to my property."

Michael rubbed the back of his neck as he sat. "Yeah. I don't really have a cabin."

Dustin's eyebrows snapped together. He forgot about their guests. "But you invited me to dinner there and all my pond stuff came from your garage."

Michael smiled, stealing Dustin's aggravation. "I thought I would just create a cabin if you came to dinner and I magicked all the things for your pond."

Dustin shook his head. He was blown away by the constant revelations. "Where have you lived all these years?"

"Right here."

Dustin's eyebrows rose. "In my house?"

Michael nodded.

It hit Dustin. Michael was the ghost. "The handprint."

A lecherous smile shaped Michael's lips. He looked at Dustin in a way that set Dustin's skin ablaze. "I had to brace myself after the show."

Heat exploded through Dustin's face.

Jonathan cleared his throat. "We're sorry to drop by unannounced like this."

Dustin tore his gaze away from Michael. "It's fine. You're always welcome here."

Tam squirmed in Risk's lap. "Yay. I can play with the fish later."

Dustin was fascinated by Tam. He was obviously an adult, but he also had the innocence of a child.

Dustin wanted to know his story.

No. You don't.

At Michael's cryptic thoughts, a wave of sadness washed over Dustin. He got the feeling Tam's life had not been a happy one.

Jonathan didn't fidget, but Dustin still got the impression he was uncomfortable. His golden gaze locked on Michael. "I was raised by my mom's mom. She told me that my mom had abandoned me at the hospital after giving birth and that she had never told anyone who my father was. I didn't know about you. If I had, I would've searched for you."

Tam cuddled close to Risk's chest. He wouldn't look directly at anyone as he added his thoughts. "I only have a vague... I don't know. It's not a memory, really. It's more like a vague idea that my mom was killed by demons. I don't really remember much of anything before getting kicked out of the Swedish pack. Everything is too bad and runs together." A sad smile touched Tam's lips. "I'm a little crazy now. Things aren't... time isn't..." Tam shrugged, as if giving up trying to explain.

Michael stared at Tam with his heart in his eyes. "I understand. My memories are the same. Madness sort of makes time less linear than it should be, and I'm no longer sure what memories are real and what are other people's dreams. When Dustin moved into this house, it took me two weeks to accept he was real. I thought I imagined him."

Dustin's heart squeezed in his chest. He couldn't imagine not seeing another soul for years. The emptiness of life had to be torture.

A sweet smile touched Tam's lips. He finally focused on Michael. "If I had known you existed, I would have found you. I've never followed the rules. Celeste wouldn't have kept me away."

Everyone nodded, as if Tam's lack of rule following was an issue. Dustin couldn't help but smile. He could see Tam being a handful.

Michael dropped his gaze to his knees. Dustin could hear his thoughts racing. He desperately wanted to be part of his sons' lives, but he feared failing them. Michael hadn't been allowed to be their father. Now they were grown, and he didn't know his place.

Finally, Michael lifted his chin. "You were both very much wanted and loved. If I had been allowed to do so, I would've been there every day. As much as I understand why I wasn't allowed to be part of your lives, I resent every second I've lost. Now you two no longer need me."

"No," Tam said, being painfully honest. "We don't need you, but we want you, and that's so much better. After all, nobody needs me for anything either, but I know I'm wanted."

Risk's arms tightened around Tam.

Tam flashed him a smile. "You don't count. You're my mate."

Dustin realized Tam responded to something Risk said mentally. It hit Dustin, he kind of needed these people he just met. No one in the human world would understand any longer. Maybe they never had.

"I was once human." Jonathan motioned toward his current form. "As you can see, I've had to learn to adjust. We won't let you flounder."

"Thank you." Dustin appreciated it more than he could say. He only had to adjust to living forever. Dustin couldn't imagine sprouting wings and fangs.

"I also grew a foot, gained about a hundred pounds, and became king in a few shorts months. It was quite the shock."

It hit Dustin. Jonathan was reading his mind.

Jonathan winced. "Sorry. It's rare for anyone to be able to block me. As a human, there's no way for you to shield your thoughts."

At Jonathan's claim, Dustin tried to be understanding. Personally, he thought having the ability to hear everyone all the time sounded like a nightmare.

"You have no idea."

A tiny snore cut through Dustin's fascination. Tam was out. A chuckle escaped Dustin before he could call it back.

"Either we're really boring, or he finally crashed."

The way Risk stared down at the mate he held twisted Dustin's heart. He wondered if Michael would ever look at him the way Risk stared at Tam.

That's how I'm looking at you now.

Dustin's gaze shot Michael's way. He was right. Michael watched him with all the love Dustin could possibly handle. Dustin wanted more. He needed Michael to unleash the heat that he barely kept contained.

Jonathan stood. "We just wanted to stop by and let you know we'd love for you to visit, and we hope it's okay if we come by sometimes too."

Guilt washed over Dustin. "You don't have to run off. I know Michael would love to spend more time with you."

Jonathan motioned Tam's way. "As you can see, the daylight hours are our usual resting hours. Not to mention, you are newly mated. You should have time alone. The newness of everything is... intense."

Dustin couldn't deny that. Still, he hoped they returned. Dustin wanted Michael to have his sons.

He knew how much he loved them and how deeply he craved being part of their lives.

Jonathan met his stare. "Thank you for that."

Dustin blinked. "For what?"

"Your thoughts," Jonathan clarified. "I can't read my father, but your thoughts are his. It matters that he wants us."

Dustin felt the pain pulsing through Michael at Jonathan calling him his father. He barely kept his knees from buckling beneath the weight of Michael's loss.

Jonathan focused on Michael. "I would very much like to hug you, if that's okay?"

Michael closed the distance between them and wrapped Jonathan in his embrace. Dustin had to look away. Jonathan could never know how much that hug meant to Michael. He had been slowly dying without his sons.

"We'll come back," Jonathan promised as Michael walked them out.

Dustin forced his feet to follow.

After they said their final goodbyes, Michael and Dustin sat on the porch swing and watched the men walk away. They disappeared inside the woods, and Dustin felt Michael's focus shift. He glanced over to find Michael staring at him.

Dustin blushed. "What?"

"You're amazing."

He wasn't, but Dustin didn't plan to argue.

"You should kiss me."

At Michael's demand, Dustin didn't hesitate. The moment their tongues met, the world disappeared. Jonathan was right. Everything was too intense for them to entertain people for long. All Dustin wanted was Michael. He didn't want to eat or sleep. Dustin didn't care if he even breathed. He needed to feel Michael's weight pinning him to the bed. Michael's love was all he required to survive.

"Dustin?"

Dustin pulled away, confused as his ex-wife's voice cut through the haze of his lust. He found Amanda standing feet away on the porch, watching him. She looked beyond shocked.

"Amanda. Hey. What are you doing here?"

She looked between Michael and him. "Um. I came to talk, but now I'm just..."

Michael stood. "I'll let you two talk. You know where I'll be."

Even with Amanda still standing there, Dustin nearly doubled over in lust. He knew exactly where Michael would be, waiting nude in Dustin's bed. He tried not to whimper as he watched Michael disappear inside. Once he was gone, Dustin forced his gaze back Amanda's way. It was odd. She felt like a stranger and he didn't remember loving her at all. Everything felt like nothing compared to what he had now.

Amanda's green eyes still flashed with confusion. "Who is that?"

"My husband." He felt Michael's possessive purr inside his head. Dustin had made Michael proud.

"Your husband? We've only been divorced a few months."

Irritation had Dustin's skin crawling. He wanted to get back to Michael. "Yet I waited a good two years longer than you."

Amanda's gaze skirted away. "I guess I deserved that one. Are you really married?"

Dustin nodded. "I am."

She rubbed her arm. "I guess that explains a lot. The whole time we were together, I always felt like you were searching for more. I just never guessed you were gay."

Dustin snorted. He saw everything as it was now. Loving Michael had nothing to do with sexuality. It went so much deeper than that, and thinking otherwise was small-minded as hell. Amanda was an idiot.

"Why are you here?"

A sardonic smile touched Amanda's lips. "It's not important. I guess I thought you'd be waiting, and we could try again. You look great, by the way."

That wasn't his doing. It seemed being an angel's mate took fifteen years off him. The rest of Amanda's claim struck him. This would likely be the last real conversation he had with his past before he disappeared into the eternal unknown. He didn't regret a thing.

"I'm sorry we wasted so many years of each other's life. You shouldn't look back."

Amanda's gaze finally collided with his. She nodded, as if she saw the truth in his eyes. There was nothing for her here, and there never would be. "I'm glad you're happy."

Dustin nodded. He watched as Amanda walked away. Then his gaze slid toward the door. His entire world waited on the other side. Dustin couldn't wait to get back to him.

⸻

WITH HIS BOTTOM LIP BETWEEN HIS TEETH, Michael stared at the bedroom doorway and waited. He could feel Dustin moving his way. Pre-cum dripped from Michael's cock onto his stomach. He had never craved anyone so much.

Dustin appeared in the doorway, and Michael stole his clothes with a single wave of his hand. If Dustin was annoyed with Michael's constant need, he didn't show it. In fact, he watched Michael with the same hunger.

"You should make love to me."

Dustin's eyebrows rose at the suggestion.

Michael knew he liked the idea. He could feel Dustin's hunger. An evil smile pulled at Michael's lips.

"What are you waiting for? Come over here and put that sexy dick in my ass."

Dustin stroked his cock as he crossed the room. "Your wish is my command."

Michael grabbed the headboard and braced himself to get fucked. He had spent too many years alone. Now he had a mate. Even though Michael knew would never be alone again, he couldn't get enough of Dustin now. They both had years of neglect to make up for. They needed the attention.

As Dustin pushed Michael's knees apart and positioned his lubed dick against Michael's asshole, he held Michael's stare. "I love you more than anything."

Michael's eyes slid closed as the power of Dustin's words washed over him. "I love you too." The confession came from the depths of Michael's soul as Dustin impaled him, making him writhe. They were one. They were whole. Michael was complete.

Please consider leaving a review at the retailer where you purchased this book. Reviews really help with a book's visibility, which allows me to continue writing more stories. Thank you, Charity.

ABOUT THE AUTHOR

Charity Parkerson is an award-winning and multi-published author with several companies. Born with no filter from her brain to her mouth, she decided to take this odd quirk and insert it in her characters.

*Eight-time Readers' Favorite Award Winner

*2015 Passionate Plume Award Finalist

*2013 Reviewers' Choice Award Winner

*2012 ARRA Finalist for Favorite Paranormal Romance

*Five-time winner of The Mistress of the Darkpath

Connect with her online:

—Sign up for my newsletter: https://sendfox.com/charityparkerson

—Join my readers' group on Facebook: http://bit.ly/CharitysTribe

—Website: charityparkerson.com

—Facebook: facebook.com/authorCharityParkerson

facebook.com/TheMenofSin

—Twitter: twitter.com/CharityParkerso

—Instagram: Instagram.com/sinnerauthor

—Bookbub: https://www.bookbub.com/authors/charity-parkerson

—Amazon page: author.to/CharityParkerson

—TikTok: http://www.tiktok.com/@charityparkerson